ARCHIBALD'S
SWISS CHEESE MOUNTAIN

"Wonderful lessons for young and old alike. Archibald's discovery of – the easiest path isn't always the best–can help children, parents and educators. I loved reading this book to my granddaughter."
—**Pat Burns,** Co-founder, Orange County Children's Book Festival
Author of *Grandparents Rock: The Grandparents Guide for the Rock-n-Roll Generation*

"A delightful story of a mouse with a big appetite for food, sights, smells and new adventures… wiser after venturing out on Swiss Cheese Mountain. A very well written cautionary tale the whole family will enjoy reading aloud."
—**Stevanne Auerbach,** Ph.D./'Dr. Toy', psychologist and author of *Smart Play Smart Toys.*

"As a professional and new grandmother, I enthusiastically recommend this book.
My grandchildren and I spend countless hours giggling over Archibald's adventures!"
—**Mari Edelman,** Ph.D., psychologist, Clinical Faculty U.C.L.A.

"A delightful cautionary tale that will enchant children who hunger
for adventure and independence, but still need to stay safe."
—**Barbara Saltzman,** Executive Director, The Jester & Pharley Phund
Publisher of *The Jester Has Lost His Jingle*

ARCHIBALD'S
SWISS CHEESE MOUNTAIN

Sylvia Lieberman

Illustrated by
Jeremy Wendell

SEVEN LOCKS PRESS
Santa Ana, California

Seven Locks Press
P.O. Box 25689
Santa Ana, CA 92799
(800) 354-5348

Individual sales: This book is available through most bookstores or can be ordered directly from Seven Locks Press at the address above.

Quantity Sales: Special discounts are available on quantity purchases by corporations, associations and others. For details, contact the "Special Sales Department" at the publisher's address above.

Printed in South Korea

Library of Congress Cataloging-in-Publication Data is available from the publisher

Design by Kira Fulks • www.kirafulks.com

ISBN: 0-9795852-5-2
       978-0-9795852-5-8

Dedication

Archibald's Swiss Cheese Mountain
is dedicated to children all over the world
who have ever felt hungry for food, love or adventure.

Acknowledgments

I wish to express my deepest gratitude for being blessed with a most devoted daughter, Dr. Carole Lieberman, and granddaughter, Tiffany Towers. They have had profound faith in my manuscript from the very beginning, and determination to propel it to a publisher. I have been immeasurably fortunate to have their unwavering support, love, warmth and inspiration.

Gratitude goes, as well, to my dear late husband, Sidney Lieberman, who was endowed with great understanding and patience towards this aspiring writer, as I spent many hours typing children's stories.

I would also like to thank my dear friend, Muriel Rosen, for her unending confidence, and my many friends who expressed delight that children everywhere will get to love Archibald as much as they do.

And finally, my eternal appreciation goes to my visionary publisher, James Riordan, and art director, Kira Fulks, of Seven Locks Press; Jeremy Wendell, a most extraordinary illustrator who captured Archibald's persona perfectly; and Michael Wright, a preeminent publicist, amongst whose clients, Archibald is honored to be included.

Foreword

I am honored and delighted to write this foreword to *Archibald's Swiss Cheese Mountain,* having lived the tale of Archie, by growing up under the nurturance of my own Momma Mouse, the author, Sylvia Lieberman. Now children everywhere will have the joy of tasting the delicious morsels of wisdom that Momma serves up in this book.

Archibald is a little mouse with a big heart and big dreams, just like little children. Indeed, children will identify with Archie, who, passionate to become 'king of the mountain', forgets his mother's cautionary advice to always "measure with your whiskers." But just as Archibald learns how to make his way in the world, overcoming obstacles and fears, this book teaches children that they, too, have the power within to master whatever challenges life puts along their path… in order to reach their 'cheese'!

Carole Lieberman, M.D., M.P.H.
Psychiatrist and Author

"Measure with your whiskers," Momma Mouse repeated.

Archibald Mouse and Momma stood beside a round hole in the wall.

"Never enter an opening, Archibald, unless your whiskers fit," Momma continued. "They are the width of your body. If your whiskers fit, so will the rest of you, my son."

Archibald was so proud of Momma. She was so wise about so many things!

This was the BIG day Archie was waiting for. Momma had been supplying him with bread and cheese crumbs for a long time. Today he would be going out into the world to find his own food.

Archibald Mouse
entered the hole,
and followed the dark path.
Momma was trailing
a short distance behind.
She watched closely,
as he sniffed,
scurried,
and
scouted.

Suddenly, out of the darkness, came a beam of light,
and the sound of heavy footsteps.

Archibald Mouse stood motionless.

He was frozen with fright.

"Fear not, Arch," Momma comforted, as she caught up to him.
"We're approaching Mr. Hochmeyer's grocery store.
There you will have no trouble keeping out of sight.
There are many boxes, barrels, and shelves to whisk behind.
If you move speedily as you were taught, you'll do just fine."

The next few hours were great fun for Archibald Mouse. Mr. Hochmeyer moved around up in front of the store, busily waiting on customers. But Archie had the best time ever, in the rear of the store. Why, he was so happy, he began to sing a jolly song, while munching a stray cookie.

"I'm sitting in Mr. Hochmeyer's store,

Surrounded by de-licious goodies galore.

I've never, ever tasted these before.

A busy little mouse am I, am I.

A busy little mouse am I."

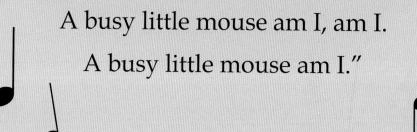

In the middle of his song, he stopped.

He had come upon two large pieces of silver foil that still had a few chunks of butter and cheese stuck to them. Mr. Hochmeyer must have discarded them, and Archibald was ever so grateful.

Just when Archie was enjoying
a great deal of freedom,
and relishing the last cube of cheese,
he heard footsteps that were
getting
a
little
too
close
for
comfort.

He climbed up
quietly
and
swiftly
to a high spot on a shelf,
and peeked out
from behind
a large can of Baked Beans.
He could see the top of
Mr. Hochmeyer's
bald head
coming up,
and going down
into a large barrel
of sauerkraut.

After several scoops of juicy, stringy sauerkraut were stuffed
into two containers, Mr. Hochmeyer's footsteps could be heard
stomping back towards the front of the store.

Archibald Mouse skipped down to nibble on a few
strings of sauerkraut that Mr. Hochmeyer had dropped
on the floor. He quickly learned about sauerkraut!
That flavorful aroma that trailed up to him,
when he was up on the high shelf was quite misleading.

It tasted tart, and so sour.

Why, it even made his nose wrinkle,
                                                    and
                                                            his whiskers twitch!

He turned around to tell Momma Mouse about this. But, to his amazement, she was nowhere to be found. No, Momma had not been around for some time. She must have seen that her young son was following her instructions quite well,
on his first day of pioneering,
and she left.

Archie realized that he was completely alone,
and slid into a sheltered corner.
He stood there, thinking.
"I'm scared and lonely," he murmured.
"But then," recovering quickly, "I've done quite
well for myself, uh, except for the sauerkraut,
of course. Yes sir, I've been ver-ry suc-cess-ful,"
he bragged out loud, while throwing his little
chest out, with great pride.

Just then,
lights started
going out
all around him.
His chest and spirit
flattened.
Things were
getting dim. With
just one small
light glowing,
Archie could see
Mr. Hochmeyer put
on his overcoat
and hat,
put the steel bar
on the rear door,
and leave through
the front
of the store.
The jingle of keys,
and a loud slam
of the door,
gave the sound of
finality to
the end of the day.

Archibald Mouse waited a moment, and then scurried behind a huge, white refrigerator. Out of the complete silence, came sounds. Many sounds.

Tick, tick, tock.
Tick, tick, tock.

Drip, drip, drop.
Drop, drop.
Drop.

Archie tried to remember if these were on the list of friendly sounds, or those that Momma Mouse warned him to beware.

The refrigerator's weary old motor
interrupted with groans, and growls, and
vibrated the entire floor.
This really shook Archie up!
But, instead of weeping with fright, he
began to giggle and dance.
That vibrating floor was tickling his toes!

"Oh my," cried Archibald Mouse.
"Everything seems to be coming alive!"

Well, everything but the radiator.
At first, it had joined in the chorus
of sounds, making a continuous sizzling,
whistling noise. But, at this moment,
the radiator gave out three coughs of steam,
and abruptly cooled off for the night.

Archibald became chilled
to the very end of his tail.

This was quite enough adventure for one small mouse.
He turned towards the hole in the corner of the wall,
thinking only of a joyful visit with Momma and family.

He was
in so great a hurry,
that he thrust himself into
the opening, happy to be leaving
all those scary sounds, cold climate,
and vibrating floor behind him.
But, there in the hole, completely
helpless he stood! His head was
on one side of the wall,
and his tail was still in
Mr. Hochmeyer's store.

Yes, Archibald's cookie and cheese-stuffed body
was stuck in that hole. No doubt about that!

Momma Mouse's advice,
"measure-with-your-whiskers,"
kept ringing in his ears.

"Yep, that's surely what I did *not* do, in my rush to leave."
He tugged and pulled desperately, with all his might,
but he just didn't seem to be getting anywhere.

"What a pred-ic-a-ment," he kept repeating.
"And it's ME, Archibald Mouse, right in the middle of it all!"
A bright thought flashed in his mind.
"My paws must be greasy from the butter and cheese.
If I could oil my tummy with my back paws,
I think I could ease myself out of here."

"You were very clever," praised Momma Mouse
after Arch told her about his experience in the hole.
"But, you were also lucky, this time. Don't count on luck too much, son,
you are much too inexperienced for that."

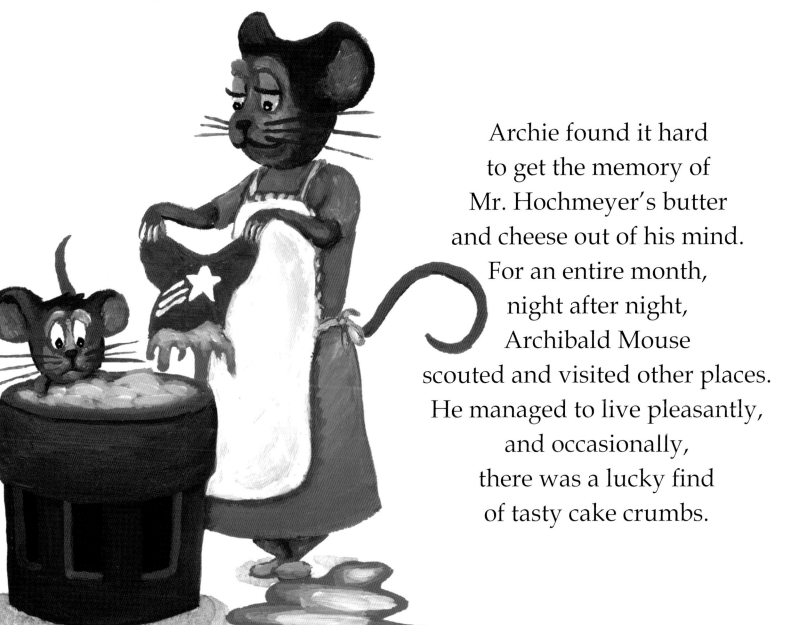

Archie found it hard
to get the memory of
Mr. Hochmeyer's butter
and cheese out of his mind.
For an entire month,
night after night,
Archibald Mouse
scouted and visited other places.
He managed to live pleasantly,
and occasionally,
there was a lucky find
of tasty cake crumbs.

Time passed. But with more brothers and sisters nibbling around, pickings grew scarce and Archie grew impatient.

Finally, one day, he gathered some courage, and told Momma Mouse firmly, "I'm off to Mr. Hochmeyer's." But, in a very short time, he returned, out of breath.

"I've made a great discovery," he panted. "Why, sitting there in a large case, in the middle of the store, is a HUGE mountain of cheese. There's enough to satisfy all of us for a very long time."

"Oh, no, I don't recommend that you go near that mountain," Momma cautioned quickly. "It is in a glass case, and you can easily be seen. You'll learn," she went on, "things within such an easy reach aren't always most desirable."

"But, but Momma,"
Archie pleaded,
"it's just some old piece of cheese
that the grocer doesn't use anymore.
It's got lots of holes in it."

Momma laughed, "That's not because it is old, Archibald, that's Swiss Cheese, and it is always made with holes in it." She began to leave, but her words trailed behind.

"No, I don't advise you try it."

"But it would make life so easy, no more hunting," Archie called after her.
"No more — ."
He stopped.
Momma was out of sight.
Archie was still curious.

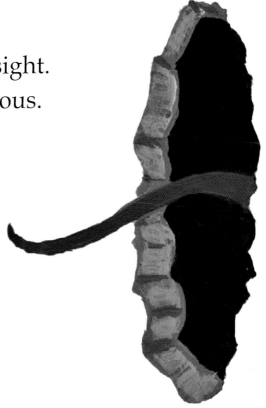

Once he reached the front area of Mr. Hochmeyer's store, he found it no problem to jump up on the counter, and reach for the pullcord of the electric fixture. He grasped it firmly, then swung like a trapeze-artist to the very top of the cheese case. Arch noted that the two air-vents on the top of the case would make a convenient entrance and exit.

"Well, here goes," he whispered, as he dived through the hole.
There he stood, proudly perched on the very top of his
Swiss Cheese Mountain.
"How lovely," he beamed, surveying all the colorful wares in the entire
store, through the glass on the case. "Yes, bee-u-tee-ful view," he grinned.
"But, enough of this, I've got a feast to enjoy."

Leisurely nibbling, Archibald ignored the drip-drop of the faucet,
the tick-tock of the clock,
and the sudden vibration of the refrigerator.
He had come to realize, these past months, that all this was harmless
to a brave little mouse. True, he was more experienced now,
but he had also grown over-confident. A new sound was coming
through all the familiar ones, but he was too busy to be disturbed.

After awhile,
Archie came out from behind
his Wonderful Mountain of Cheese,
just for a casual yawn and stretch.
He pushed his cute little nose against
the glass case, to get a closer look at the view.

Archibald gasped! Two glowing green eyes stared back at him.

He was too frightened
to look again.
He just
squeezed
himself
into the nearest hole
in the cheese
that could
accommodate him.

He curled up his tail, pulled in his ears, and tried to remain motionless.
But, Archie's heart pounded, and his whiskers quivered with fright. Much
excitement could be heard going on outside of that glass case, but he wouldn't
dare look out. "Trapped and cornered am I," he thought. "But safe, as long as that
Thing-a-ma-jig with the piercing green eyes remains outside." Once more, there
was a lot of noise and fussing at the glass case. With a sudden recognition that
this was a sound to BEWARE, the mystery was solved. "Meow, meow, scratch,
scratch," were now furiously coming through to Archie's ears.

"That's Mr. Hochmeyer's c-c-cat!" Archibald stuttered. "Oh, n-n-no!"

He squeezed deeper into his Swiss Cheese refuge.
But it wasn't long after a few more attempts that Green Eyes
gave up and went away. Archibald Mouse remained in his
hideout, calming down, from such a frightening experience.
He was so limp, and tired. His confidence was so shaken,
that he sat worrying if he'd ever make
the trip back home safely.

Mr. Hochmeyer's keys rattled at the door.
"My, it must be morning already," thought Archie.

At this very moment his weary eyes closed.
He hadn't had a wink of sleep, and his eyelids became
much too heavy for a little mouse to keep open another minute.
Archibald Mouse fell into an exhaustive slumber!

He probably would have
remained inside the cheese all day,
catching up on his lost sleep,
but suddenly he was awakened.

He was being moved bodily.

Peeking out from a crack in the cheese, Archie
saw Mr. Hochmeyer's hand.
Arch realized that he and the cheese were
being lifted
from its case onto the counter-top.

Mr. Hochmeyer reached for a shiny, sharp knife.
"And do you want it sliced thick or thin, today, Mrs. Nelson?"
Mr. Hochmeyer questioned.

"Wh-wh-wh-what? Oh my," Arch muttered to himself,
as the words drifted to him through the holes in the cheese.

Quickly, he ventured into a trail, which led him deeper into the
center of the Cheese Mountain. He still was not sure that he
was safe from the sharp edge of that knife. "What if Mrs. Nelson
wants a lot of cheese today?" was his gloomy thought.

Mr. Hochmeyer sharpened the big knife carefully
on a smooth, gray stone. From his hiding place, Archibald could just
about make out the muffled sounds of Mrs. Nelson's voice.
"I've changed my mind, Mr. Hochmeyer. I think I'll bring home
cream cheese to my family, today." She pointed, and continued,
"The kind you have in the other case."
"Whatever you wish, Mrs. Nelson," Mr. Hochmeyer replied,
sliding Archie and the Cheese Mountain back into place.
"Whew!" Archie whistled, "That was close!"

Mr. Hochmeyer was slicing
and weighing the cream cheese,
and busily speaking to Mrs. Nelson.
He was discussing the price of bologna,
a new shipment of imported sardines,
and the weather, of course.
Arch took this opportunity to flee from
his wonderful, but dangerous spot.

Once out of the exit, he swiftly
scurried along a very high shelf,
hidden from view by a long row of tall
jars. Archibald Mouse reached
the very end of the long shelf.

He poked his head out around
a large jar of bright, red,
Maraschino Cherries.
After one last yearning look at his
beautiful Swiss Cheese Mountain,
Archie sighed.

He contentedly headed for home,
whisker-measuring
all along the way.